MR. DEATH
Four Stories

MR. DEATH

Four Stories

by Anne Moody

Foreword by John Donovan

Harper & Row, Publishers

New York, Evanston,

San Francisco, London

38329

FIRST EDITION

juc 5.95   12-23-75

Dedicated to Sascha, with special thanks to Claudie who typed and retyped the book in manuscript. To Ellen Rudin, my editor, for her sharp and insightful comments. And to Warren—a special thanks for three weeks last November.

Foreword

Four stories. Each is a tragedy. While death is part
of each of these four stories, it's misleading to dwell
on the pitiable deaths in "Mr. Death"; the abrupt-
ness and violence of the deaths in "The Cow"; the
gruesome naturalness of the deaths in "Bobo"; and
on the masks people assume in "All Burnt Up" to
protect themselves from deaths that are closest to
them. Wait a minute. Wait several. Read beyond
the deaths. Read these stories slowly. Inside each
of them—whatever their surfaces may suggest—the
attempt Anne Moody makes is to help us understand the nature of love. Beyond the violent deaths
so much a part of each of these stories, *feel* the lives
of those most affected by these events: Rodney
with his dream in "Mr. Death"; the childlike Truelove, and her innocent, dumb child Louella, in "The
Cow"; the German shepherd and its victims in
"Bobo"; and Poochie, slyly devoted to a dead
woman who made her *feel* a person in "All Burnt
Up." In each instance of death that Anne Moody

depicts here, her hope seems to be to make us think of the passions, centering on the infinite variety of ways that love can manifest itself, that have brought about the final, terrible revelations that the concluding episodes in each story reveal.

Theater lore tells us that when the ancient Greeks went to see their plays—their greatest plays, those works that have lived through the ages and are performed even today—it was to experience a catharsis. My simple little dictionary defines *catharsis* as "a purifying or purging of the emotions through the effect of art, as through the arousal of pity and terror on witnessing tragic drama."

Consciously or otherwise, Anne Moody is calling on us to experience a kind of catharsis in reading her four stories. They will frighten and horrify you; they will make your life richer than it was.

—John Donovan

Mr. Death

I am Rodney Weatherspoon. Tomorrow I will be thirteen. My mother died four years ago when I was nine. Last night I had a dream which made me realize that I too died early that morning around five o'clock. Pa did too, but he hasn't realized it yet. He still doesn't know that Ma is dead. At least he hasn't let himself know it. Even though it's been four years ago that Ma's been gone, everything in the house is exactly the same way it was when she was alive.

Pa locked his bedroom door the day they took Ma's body out. It's been locked ever since. When he goes in he unlocks it and locks it right back behind him. When he comes out he locks it and it's left that way the rest of the day. No one else has been in that room since the day they took Ma's body away—not even me.

I wonder why he doesn't let anyone in there. Sometimes I think Ma is still alive. I didn't see them take her away and at the funeral her coffin was sealed. Grandma said that she had wasted away so. . . . And another thing. I hear Pa in there talking to her just as though she was still alive. You see, Ma was sick for six months before she finally died. And during the entire six months Pa was always asking her:

"Rosetta, is you warm enough? Just as soon as spring comes um gonna undo the walls in here and put in another layer of Sheetrock."

I don't ever hear Ma answering back or anything, but before she died she was too weak to talk anyway. So it's possible she could still be in there. Then too, he's always chopping wood. When Ma died we had only one woodshed, now we have three. And he keeps the fire going in the fireplace in their room every day of the year all day long. Whenever I am outside in the yard, or on my way from school or someplace, I see smoke oozing out of the chimney—even in ninety-degree weather.

In all the four years, he has never looked at another woman. He doesn't have any friends and I don't either. He keeps me so busy I don't have time

4

to have any. As soon as I get in from school, I have to chop wood, feed the chickens, slop the hogs, eat supper, do my lessons and go to sleep. Things were different when Ma was alive. I used to go down the road and play with Billy Jo every day for an hour or so after school. Now I hardly ever see him. When I am sick with flu or something Pa lets him come and take my assignments to school for me, and when he is sick I stop in and do the same for him.

Oh! I have missed the Sundays when Ma would sit out on the lawn and teach me and Billy Jo how to draw and paint with water colors. She was real good at it and she said I had a lot of talent and that one day I might be a famous artist. But I don't draw or paint anymore either. Pa says it's too sissy. Once I wrote a composition in school that was so good my teacher gave me an A on it. She wrote on it that I could possibly end up being a writer one day. When I showed it to Pa that evening he said:

"You can't make any money being a writer, son. You better think about being an insurance man or something. Looka that big fine house old Will got himself down the road. And he done got it out of the money he made selling fools like us a lousy insurance policy."

The only thing Pa's done that's given me any

5

pleasure since Ma's been gone was to give me this tape recorder last Christmas. I know he gave it to me so that it would occupy my time so I wouldn't have any need to bring Billy Jo or anybody here to disturb his peace of mind. All the same I have fun with it. I just lay up here in bed and talk in it all the time just like I'm doing now. I tape stories from the radio like "The Shadow," record poems and stories that I write myself and tape just about all of my dreams, especially the interesting ones.

Last night's dream was one of the clearest I have had in a long time. I have had a lot of strange dreams since Ma's death, but this one made me see the light—that I have been dying ever since. In it, Pa and I were walking down a long lonely road. It was wide and well kept. There were no ugly shacks or houses to spoil the beauty of the grass and trees. Even though there were no signs on the road, indicating its name, and even though I was sure I had never been on it before, it looked familiar. It was like a state highway connecting two or more states. Pa and I have been on all the state highways around here and I remember each one of them. But this one was not like any of the others. It seemed to be something out of my past, something that had been there since I was four or five. I knew its every detail. All along the bank next to the road, way back to the trees in the distance, was the healthiest dark green grass I have ever seen.

I remember as a child sitting on the lawn playing with my toys and watching Ma and Pa doing the gardening. Pa would oil up the old rusty lawn mower and sweat like crazy until all the grass was cut. He went over and over it until it was short and neat. In my dream, the grass along the road was the same, short and freshly cut, but it had a peculiar odor that was all its own. Other grass did not smell that way, yet it was the smell of grass. It was so pretty. I was tempted to touch it to see if it was real. But it wasn't necessary. I knew it was real. It was so real that in comparison Pa and I appeared unreal. And I very strongly felt that we did not belong there—not the way we were. Our appearance seemed to cast a dark and sinister look over the landscape.

Anyway it was getting dark and I have always felt that during that time of day all things seem to be coming to an end. But more than the day or that beautiful landscape or anything else, Pa and I seemed to be the only things that was really coming to an end. The scene surrounding us looked as though it had always been there and always would, more or less just like it was. I couldn't relate to it and I could see that Pa couldn't either. I felt myself disintegrating—coming apart.

I stepped right out of the skin of the boy. He was no longer me and the man was no longer Pa. But Pa didn't step out like me. He remained inside of the man. Now I was standing there looking at the father and his son, observing them along with the highway and grass and all. I saw then that even though the scene was so beautiful, there was something unnatural about it. The highway was so wide and long that in proportion the father and son looked like little ants crawling along it. Now it seemed to be growing longer and longer and getting wider and wider. I began to think that I was imagining things. But after a while I saw that it was actually happening. It was expanding.

Now I forced myself to look more closely at the father and son, trying to decide who they were and did I know them. Even though I'd just stepped right out of the skin of that boy, they were strangers to me. The man was slightly graying and looked to be in his mid-forties, same as Pa, while the son was barely in his teens, same as me. They were carrying fishing poles. They looked very tired as if they had been fishing for days. I thought that they had probably been wandering for miles along some creek somewhere. They walked and walked on the road but never seemed to make any progress. They were always in the same spot.

Suddenly there was a car moving up the road. Because the highway was so large, it too looked very small, like the father and son. The car crept slowly up behind them. They did not see it yet. I hoped that it would pick them up. Then they would be gone and I could see if the landscape would change. When the car came right up beside them, the father waved for it to stop. It went straight past them. Suddenly it stopped and waited. The father and son walked towards it. They walked so slowly to it that I couldn't tell if they were approaching it cautiously or whether they were just too tired to move any faster. There was something queer about the car. It was not like a regular limousine, not like the ones I saw when Pa and I visited Chicago. It was black and exceptionally long, with four rows of seats. There was something so strange and compelling about it that I completely forgot about the landscape and joined the father and son who were just getting into the third row.

I got into the last row so I could watch everything. Although I was right on top of the father and the son, they didn't even know I was there. Or was I there?

There were three seats in each of the four rows. The father and the son occupied the two end seats in front of me. There was a huge, slightly slumping figure in the middle seat of the well-spaced second row. And the driver's seat was occupied by a chauffeur in full uniform.

It was very dark inside the car, almost too dark.

Just as I began to wonder why it was so much darker in the car than it was outside, I noticed that the curtains were drawn at every window except the driver's seat. The whole inside of the car was upholstered in deep maroon velvet. There was a sweet smell in the air. I felt a strong breeze even though all the windows were closed. It felt as though it came from outside, but I knew that was not so; there had not been any wind outside at all. Perhaps, I thought, there is an air conditioner. I looked and didn't see one.

Now looking at the father and son again, I saw that the father looked so frightened of the big slumping man in front of him. He was seated so he could see the man's face. I wished he would turn around so I could see him. But he just sat there. Certainly there was something about him that was terrifying the father. But the son seemed merely curious. Then he turned. My God! I tell you I had never seen such a weird-looking man! His face was all wrinkled—dry like the skin of a turtle. It was the oldest-looking skin I have ever laid eyes on. The sight of it made me tremble with fear.

"We . . ." the father began very authoritatively, then paused and began again more deferentially. "We . . . would like to get off at the first . . . the first intersection."

The strange face slowly began to break out into

a long narrow smile as if to acknowledge the deference paid to it.

"I am Mr. Death," it said in a deep rasping tone that seemed to come from everywhere. "Who might *you* be?" he continued, turning his head from the father to the son.

I was positive he said his name was Mr. Death, but I didn't want to believe it. However when I looked at the father and saw the horror in his eyes, I figured I had heard right.

"Th . . . th . . . that is my son," the father said. "My name is . . . is . . ."

Mr. Death cut him off as if he were not interested in who he was.

"Son," he said, patting the seat beside him, "would you like to sit next to me?"

The boy smiled acceptingly as if to say it would be a great honor. But just as he was about to move, his father pushed him back against the seat.

"My son will remain with me," said the father, then added faintly, "if you don't mind?" Just then the father sounded like Pa. At Ma's funeral one of my aunts was talking to me about living with them now that Ma was dead. And Pa said to her, "Rodney will remain with me if you don't mind," in the same tone the father spoke to Mr. Death. Anyway, Mr. Death said, "Whatever you like," and turned abruptly in his seat.

We moved along for some time in complete silence. The chauffeur never said a word and never turned his head around. He never moved. I couldn't see his hands moving on the steering wheel. I didn't even see a steering wheel. There must have been a steering wheel because certainly the car was moving. Or was it moving? I was just beginning to wonder if the chauffeur or the car were real when Mr. Death suddenly spoke out.

"We must stop here for a moment," he said, addressing everyone in the car.

Before the words were out of his mouth the car was swerving off the road, as if his voice were directing it. It went down an embankment and came to rest right at the edge of the woods. I had to pee very badly so I quickly got out of the car and ran deep into the woods. Once I started peeing, it echoed through the woods like a distant waterfall. I was embarrassed. I knew they could hear me, or thought they could. I tried to stop in order to go deeper into the woods, but I had held it too long, it was beyond stopping now.

Coming out of the woods, I saw the father, the son and Mr. Death standing with their backs to me facing a square piece of earth, about eight feet in diameter, from which a thin layer of grass-covered earth had been sliced. There were four square posts firmly planted, one in each corner of the recently scraped earth. Mr. Death was gesturing with his hands as if he were explaining something to the father and son. I was too far away to hear what was being said. As I moved closer to them, I could see that the soil was dark and rich-looking. Full of curiosity, I moved quickly towards them. Mr. Death was lightly waving his hand and saying something to the son.

Looking up, I saw for the first time that the four posts were supporting the layer of earth and grass that had been removed from the ground below. It was directly above the plot, like the overhead canopy on Grandma's four-poster bed. I couldn't imagine what it was.

Coming up behind them I heard Mr. Death say, "Go on, go on. . . ."

The son began to move towards the plot but the father stuck out his arm, preventing him from doing so. Mr. Death, showing his displeasure with the father, turned to leave immediately. The father followed. The son, defying his father's order, sneaked onto the soil. The father, unaware of this, continued to follow Mr. Death, as if he were drawing him away, leaving the son to carry out his order. The son ran on and off the plot in a mischievous way, then fell in line behind the father as if he had done nothing. It seems funny but as the boy ran on and off the plot, I seemed to be running with him, like his shadow. But at the same time, I was watching him, walking behind him, following the father and Mr. Death to the car.

As Mr. Death came up to the car his door swung open without his even touching it. He waited until everyone was in, then gracefully seated himself. All the doors closed simultaneously and the car took off. The chauffeur still had not moved.

The "first intersection" the father wanted to get out at never came. The car moved along for quite some time. All the while the father looked anxiously through the windshield as if at any moment the intersection would appear. Soon it was completely dark. The lights of the car beamed brightly down on the road and the seated figures ahead of me were only silhouettes outlined against the glare of the headlights.

Before we knew it the car was swerving off the road again. It came right up to the base of a building and stood before what appeared to be a garage door. The building loomed up so unexpectedly that I didn't get a chance to see it in its entirety, but from the size of the door confronting us, it appeared to be gigantic. Sitting there, I first thought that we had driven up to a huge restaurant. The car was immediately filled with a variety of delicious-smelling odors as if they came from some fancy restaurant.

The garage door suddenly curled up into its roof like a tongue. The car entered and I discovered we were not in a garage but smack in the middle of a large kitchen. A big fat lady cook, dressed in a white uniform all splotched with food, silently moved around a steam table in the middle of the floor, stirring and dipping long-handled spoons into deep oval pots submerged in the steaming water. She acted as if she didn't see us even though she turned in our direction several times. I thought it funny that our being in the middle of her kitchen in that weird car didn't evoke more of a response. Then I realized we weren't in the car. We *had* entered in the car—I was sure of that. But now we were just standing there.

The food smelled so good the son began to slobber at the mouth like a dog. The father looked at him scoldingly, the same as Pa always looks at me when we're eating out by some of our relatives or somewhere. Mr. Death noticed the father's reproving glance and showed his displeasure by a slight but significant raise of his eyebrows. Then he motioned us towards a door leading to a moderate-sized room. We entered and before us stood a long table draped to the floor with a more-than-white tablecloth. It was surrounded by about two dozen chairs. This was the only furniture in the room.

Standing at the head of the table, Mr. Death motioned to the father to take the chair opposite him at the other end, patting the seat next to him for the son.

"You will dine with me," Mr. Death said, "and then you will spend the night."

"No, no . . ." The father began to object but, pausing to reconsider, he nodded his head submissively as if to say, "If you so wish, we'll spend the night." Again he sounded like Pa.

Mr. Death, obviously enjoying the control he exercised over the father, indulged in one of his broad, slow, cynical smiles as he looked at the father's bowed, balding, perspiring head. The end of the table where he sat faced the door of the kitchen. He merely looked in the direction of the door and the cook suddenly appeared with a long rolling serving tray loaded with two tiers of delectable-looking food. She quickly circled the table and as she did so the food jumped in place all over the table without her touching one dish. She was gone just as suddenly as she had entered.

Mr. Death nodded and began eating, permitting everyone else to do the same. Instead of picking up a fork and waiting for food to be passed like everyone else, like I always do when I'm eating with Pa or relatives, I found myself walking down the long table among all the heaping plates taking whatever

I liked, but no one seemed to notice me. Again, I wondered if I was actually there—but then I knew I must be because I was tasting and eating the food. I couldn't figure out how I was walking on the table because every conceivable space was taken up. I just seemed to be going in and out among the mounds of dishes on some invisible road.

I was so wrapped up in gorging myself with one tasty dish after another that I forgot all about Mr. Death and his dinner guests, until his deep voice startled me. I hadn't realized it was so silent until he spoke: "I will show you where you are to bed tonight," he said, rising and moving towards a door I hadn't noticed before. I was sure that wall was solid before he had spoken.

We walked down a narrow hallway with countless doors leading off to unknown rooms. In the middle of the corridor he stopped and, looking at the father, said, "*You* will occupy this room."

The father put his arm around his son and stood with his back to the door as if the two of them were about to bid Mr. Death good night. But Mr. Death smiled and said, "Son, follow me."

"No, no, I prefer my son to share my room with me," the father pleaded. This time he sounded like Pa did the time we spent the night at Aunt Esther's when I'd wanted to sleep on a pallet in front of the fireplace.

"That is im*poss*ible, there being only one small bed in each room. I have a special room for him," Mr. Death said, walking away with the boy following hypnotically. The father looked pale and worried but he knew he dared not object so he turned reluctantly and went into his room.

Mr. Death led the boy all the way to the last room at the end of the hallway. I wondered where my room was, but he didn't offer me one. I wandered back down the hallway with the intention of occupying whichever room I liked. But then I turned and quickly ran after Mr. Death. I wanted to see where he was going. I reached him just as he was leaving the hallway through a thick door resembling the entrance to a vault. We entered a vast, glittering, chandeliered, ornate room with marble steps leading to a high mezzanine, so high that from where I stood I could only see the undersurface of its floor. Everything was so gleaming clean and polished-looking.

Mr. Death proceeded right up the marble steps. I was tempted to examine the room more closely but instead I ran up the steps behind him. When I reached the mezzanine I immediately saw six doctors wearing masks hovering over a figure lying on an operating table. Several nurses ran back and forth out of adjacent rooms. I could not see who was on the table so I moved in closer, right among

18

the doctors. They didn't notice me. They just kept talking among themselves.

The operating table at first seemed to be higher than me and I had to look up at it, but looking at the person lying on it, I was now looking down. The patient was Ma. She lay there dead. I'm sure she was dead. I wondered what the doctors were doing about to operate on her if she was dead. Yet they were just as busy as a bunch of doctors working on a live patient, trying to save her. I stood there praying for Ma, hoping that the doctors would be able to save her.

All of a sudden I heard a heavy door squeaking. I knew it was the vaulted door I had entered with Mr. Death even though I had not heard it squeak before. Turning and looking down the marble steps to the door, I saw that I was right. Two doctors were now entering the room with a tray of freshly extracted human organs. Immediately I knew it must be the organs from the son because they looked small. As the two doctors came up the steps with the organs, I dashed past them down the steps, through the vaulted door towards the son's room. Coming up to the door I saw what appeared to be a piece of bloody liver lying on the floor in front of the door.

Instead of opening the door and going in, I whirled and ran back through the vaulted door, up the steps behind the doctors. I didn't follow them all the way up, but stood in the middle of the steps and tried to figure out what was going on. Finally I went on up the steps, intending to see what was happening on the operating table. But when I got there, the doctors, the operating table and all their paraphernalia were gone. Ma was now in the middle of the room lounging on a love seat, dressed in a long flowing negligee that fell in silky folds to the floor. It was the same gown she wore the last time I saw her before she died. She looked as if she was sleeping. I stood watching her, trying to determine if she was alive now. But before I could come to any conclusions she opened her eyes and regally rose to her feet, then slowly glided by me, her negligee flowing out behind her as if she was moving in a strong breeze.

I ran downstairs through the thick vaulted doorway, past the son's room with the bloody liver still lying before it, not stopping until I reached the father's room. Now I was thinking it was Pa. I would go tell him Ma was alive. But just as I approached the door he wrenched it open and ran out of it down towards his son's room. Seeing the liver on the floor, he turned and ran the whole length of the hallway out the door at the other end. I followed him, still thinking he was Pa. Outside the building, which I saw for the first time was a castle, was the highway. The father ran wildly down it, crying and heaving at the chest. I stayed right behind him even though he ran much faster than I knew I could run.

Soon he neared the plot of earth we had been to before. Mr. Death's big limousine was parked there. Just as the father approached, the car pulled away. As Mr. Death passed us he flashed a broad smile that said, "It's all over with, you fool." I'm sure the father read just that into the smile, for now he began crying hysterically and running towards the plot. Now I noticed the posts were disappearing down into the earth, and just as the father reached it, the canopy of grass-covered earth sealed it. The father fell on top of it in a fit of uncontrollable sobs. It *was* Pa! And he just lay there on the ground crying like he did the day Ma died.

"Sheriff Prichard, how long do you think they've been dead?" Old Lady Weatherspoon, Rodney's grandma, asked as she stood bracing herself against Old Man Weatherspoon and the foot of Rodney's bed. She, along with three other relatives, stood staring down at Rodney's and his father's lifeless, almost headless bodies sprawled in a pool of blood in Rodney's bed.

"Well, it's hard to say," Sheriff Prichard answered. "It seems as though that boy, Billy Jo,

Hackard's boy down the road, stopped in to see if Rodney was sick or something. He was the one who discovered them. His ma, who came and told me, said the boy was so upset that all he could do was convey to her that they'd both been shot in the head. Then she got in her car and almost killed herself on her way into town to tell me. I just known bout it three hours ago. Soon as I done heard, I sent for you. My speculation is they've been dead for about a week. Miss Hackard told me that Billy Jo says Rodney ain't been to school in about a week."

"I jus knew something was gonna happen. Ever since Rosetta died that son of mine been completely outta his mind. It jus wasn't healthy the way he depended upon Rosetta. And for the last four years he's been completely lost without her," she said between sobs. "And I felt so sorry for po Rodney," she continued. "He he heee he—Bud never let him go anywhere and the po child had no friends. He gave him that tape recorder last Christmas and po Rodney spent every penny he got his hands on buyin tapes. Whenever I was here he wanted money for them tapes. . . ."

"Y'all come out heah," Sheriff Prichard said. "Listen to this. It seems as though Rodney just taped it fore he killed hisself. It'll help you understand what really did happen. My theory is—and

um gonna go into town and git the coroner out here—Rodney had this bad dream and went down in the cellar and got the shotgun and sat up here in bed and killed hisself. Then Bud came home and found that Rodney had blown his brains out and killed hisself."

Old Lady Weatherspoon started crying more than before and Sheriff Prichard took her around the waist, saying:

"Here. Y'all just come on out here in the living room and I'll bring this tape machine out there, then y'all kin listen to it while I go into town and git that coroner."

Once Old Lady and Old Man Weatherspoon and the other few relatives were seated in the living room, Sheriff Prichard brought in the tape recorder and switched it on.

I am Rodney Weatherspoon. Tomorrow I will be thirteen. My mother died four years ago when I was nine. Last night I had a dream which made me realize that I too died early that morning around five o'clock. . . .

The relatives sat quietly sobbing and listening.

The Cow

Henry, if you don't get out there and get that damn cow out of that garden, I'll take this shotgun and blow its head off.

The cow was given to them as a wedding present. Ideally it would have been the perfect gift for Truelove and Henry, if only it had been given by someone other than Henry's mother whom Truelove couldn't stand. Truelove was pregnant when she and Henry got married and the cow was pregnant when it was given to them.

Truelove was certain that the cow was given as a testament of her mother-in-law's feelings towards her. She knew her mother-in-law looked down on her because she was pregnant when she married Henry. She knew also that his mother didn't even believe that the baby was for him. The baby, in her estimation, could have been for any man, just like the cow's calf could have been for any of the three bulls in her stable. Truelove knew that even though her mother-in-law was aware of the fact that she had been dating Henry for three years prior to their marriage and that she had never known another man the whole time, she still thought it immoral of her to have slept with Henry before she was officially his bride.

Truelove didn't only resent her giving them a pregnant cow, but she resented most of all the type of cow she gave. Any other cow in the world would have been better than this one. Why could she not have given them just a nice little simple dumb cow? It would have been easy for her to do. She had plenty of nice simple dumb ones. But instead she gave them the most mischievous, discontented, humanlike, rebellious cow this side of China. Not only was it rebellious, but it acted as though it had been specially trained to bug her.

They had only had the cow three weeks and already it had broken down the hogpen, letting the hogs out to run wild in the nearby woods. It took Henry three days to catch them and return them to their pen. A few days later she knocked down the prop of the clothesline and was found eating the wet sheets. And just the other day when they had company, she stood right in the front yard smelling up the porch where they sat with their guests. When Henry chased her out of the yard as the guests were about to leave, she came back and shitted on the front walk, forcing the guests to use the driveway as an exit. Now she had broken into the garden and was eating the greens like they were specially planted for her. Truelove looked at it as Henry led it out of the garden and wondered what it would find to do to bug her the coming day.

"First thing tomorrow um gonna go up there and ask Miss Phillips if I can keep this damn cow on that there land of hers," Henry said, gesturing to the land across the creek in back of their house. "It ain't doin nothin but goin to waste anyhow."

"It'd just be a waste of time," Truelove said. "You know that stingy-ass old sow ain't gonna let you."

"We gotta do somethin wit this heah damn cow. You's gittin too big to be runnin after her and draggin her all the way up to that pond. It'll take her three months to eat her way through all them weeds and vines back there."

The five acres of rich land stretched out in back of their house had become something of a pipe

29

dream since Henry had tried to buy a piece of it two years ago. He'd hoped to build their house on it and leave enough for Truelove to have a good-sized garden and front lawn. But Miss Phillips wouldn't sell it to him. Instead she sold him the acre and a half of sand on the edge of the road. Every time he came home and saw Truelove out there fiddling around in that little twelve-by-twelve-by-twenty triangle of a garden of hers, when more than five acres of good rich land was going to seed right in his back yard, he got furious. Once Miss Phillips came down and put up a big POSTED sign directly in front of their back door.

"It ain't no need in the world for you to put that there sign up," Henry said, jumping the little creek in back of his house. "You kin jus take it right down."

"Why should I?" Miss Phillips asked. "This is my property and I intend for it to stay just that."

"If you don't take it down," Henry shouted, "I will," jerking the sign off the fence. "Son of a bitch!" he yelled, slinging the sign into the creek and licking blood from the thumb he'd pricked on the barbed wire.

Miss Phillips looked at him as if he was mad, grabbed her walking cane and began to hop away as quickly as possible.

"You ain't got nothin to worry bout," Henry

30

hurled at her back. "I know dis heah land is yo's. If you gotta put up that damn sign why don't you put it up on the road so people who don't know whose property it tis will know to stay offa it? Another thing, them chaps coming in from school always horsing around out there and losing balls and things, may be you jus betta git yo'self a couple of them damn German shepherds tuh keep dem out."

Miss Phillips had not spoken to him since the business about the sign, and Henry dreaded the thought of asking her for any kind of favor, but for Truelove's sake—for Truelove's sake, he'd do just about anything.

The very next day on his way to work he stopped by and asked. She seemed pleased that he'd given her the opportunity to say no to him. But in spite of her he was glad he'd done it. He would certainly not waste any more time thinking about it as a possibility. For he now realized he'd been thinking about that land a long time. He knew he'd even bought that triangle of sand from Miss Phillips, who was sixty-seven, thinking she'd be dead in a few years anyway, and her daughter, who had no use for the five acres across the creek, would sell it to him for next to nothing. But from the contemptuous look Miss Phillips gave him when she said, "I'm not about to sell that piece of land to

nobody and if I did you'd be the *last* person I'd sell
it to," he figured she'd live another sixty years just
to spite him.

Truelove, who was forced, out of poverty, to sub-
sist on a diet of carbohydrates and fats, was over-
weight to begin with. She was only three months,
but she looked as if she was already about to get
down. On her last checkup her doctor informed her
that she had gained twenty pounds. She resented
him when he so casually told her to cut down on
the starches and sugars, as if she was Lady Vander-
bilt or Mrs. Rockefeller or some other woman with
millions. "Anyway, how can I cut down on my
sugars and starches when all I got to eat is red
beans and rice and a side of pork every now and
then?" she asked the doctor. And she thought,
"Anyway, whattaya know about bein poor when
you was born into all your daddy's money and
never had to hit a lick at a snake?"

She remembered Aunt Kellogg, the midwife who
had delivered her and the rest of her mother's
children. She'd been dead four years now. She
delivered her last baby two days before she died
at the age of sixty-eight. In fact, she delivered practically all the black babies in Bakersville, the little
town Truelove was brought up in twenty miles
away, and in all of the shacks and little towns for

miles around. "Aunt Kellogg never worried about how fat anybody got and the best thing about it, she ain't never charged no more than five dollars to deliver a baby," Truelove said to herself. "Already we owe this big gyp a hundred and twenty-five dollars and gotta pay two hundred and fifty dollars for the damn delivery. Shit, wit that lil bit o money Henry's makin at the sawmill, we'll be payin him off for the next five years."

Every day Truelove spent most of her time sitting on the porch rocking in an old squeaky English rocker given to her by Miss Calhoun, a lady she worked for in Bakersville. She could not stand the stuck-up niggers living in the quarters where she now lived with Henry. She sometimes even hated the little tiny three-room house Henry'd built for them. Even worse than being on a barren sandy plot, it was situated right in the angle of a ninety-degree fork in the road and all the traffic in and out of the quarters passed by there. It was so close to the road that when cars came speeding by, they'd pop rocks all the way up on the porch. Sometimes teen-age boys, who had just gotten their licenses and were always showing off, would drive fast right to the curve, then turn all of a sudden, sending up a shower of rocks clean over the house.

The dust was impossible. Not only was it dangerous for Truelove to breathe in as she sat there rocking all day, but her wash always got ruined. Her white clothes were bleached and white as snow when she hung them out, but by the time they were dry and she brought them in they were brown. It got so bad, she dyed all of her white sheets blue but finally it hit her that whether the sheets were white or blue, they were still dirty when she brought them in.

She longed to be back in Bakersville, in the big old farmhouse sitting in the middle of a pasture surrounded by woods. She'd spent the first sixteen years of her life there. She remembered all the fun she'd had in its spacious living room and the times when all the family were gathered together around the huge fireplace cutting up and enjoying each other. Most of all she missed the people she knew, going to church every Sunday and fishing in her favorite creek back of the old house she grew up in.

Since her belly was so big and she was burdened with extra weight, Truelove tired very easily. Most of the time she just kept the cow on a long rope tied to one of the posts supporting the roof of the porch. She felt sorry for the cow tied there in the hot sun all day. To make things easier for Truelove, Henry'd gotten into the habit of taking his sling blade to work with him. Then on his way home in the evening he'd stop and cut grass all the way along the twenty-five-mile stretch of road on his way back home. Sometimes he drove up to the house with the back of the pickup loaded down with grass. And all the next day Truelove'd feed the cow until the grass was gone.

Even though the cow was pregnant same as herself, Truelove could see it was tolerating the sun better than she ever could. For all the trouble the cow was constantly causing. Truelove subconsciously wished—and the wish wasn't really so subconscious—it'd be miserable there in the hot sun. She couldn't stand seeing it so relaxed and cool-looking while she sat there on the porch in the shade fanning and sweating up a storm. She'd never been so miserable in her whole life. But she'd never been four months pregnant in July in her whole life either. For that matter neither had the cow. She was only two and a half years old. This would be her first calf and she was lying out there in the boiling sun as though she'd already had fifty. Occasionally she'd whisk her tail from side to side to rid herself of the flies that were pestering her. But mostly she just lay there chewing and chewing on her cud—chewing and swallowing and coughing up the grass until it was soft and swallowed for good. All that chewing got on Truelove's nerves and she was usually glad when it was evening and she'd drag the cow up to the pond by the highway and let it graze on the green grass there.

Since she waited until the sun was just about down, the journey to the pond wasn't as bad as it might have been. Besides, she always took along her hook and stopper. And every other day she'd come home with a good mess of perch. Old Man Thompson would turn over in his grave if he knew she was fishing in that pond. When she had asked Old Lady Thompson if she could let her cow graze there, she told her, "Long as you don't do any fishin, it's all right with me. That pond was the only peace Will had fo he died, and ah don't want nobody disturbin it long as ahm livin." So every day when she'd pass Old Lady Thompson standing there in the window looking out to make sure she wasn't bringing along a fishing pole, Truelove would give her that same grateful wave, thanking her for being so nice and letting her cow eat the grass there by the pond. In the beginning, once Truelove'd passed Old Lady Thompson's house, she'd used any stick she'd find in the woods near the pond to fish with. But then Old Lady Thompson, who was a lonesome old pain in the ass, would come down every other day and talk to Truelove just about the whole time she was there. So now Truelove got scared and didn't even use a pole to fish with. Instead, underneath her smock next to her big pregnant belly she carried her line wrapped around a short stick ten inches or so long and that was all she used. Whenever she'd see Old Lady Thompson coming, she'd stick the stick down in the mud at the edge of the pond, completely concealing it under the water. Then she'd walk over to greet her as if she had just been doing nothing more than sitting there contemplating the ripples.

One day Old Lady Thompson stayed there chatting so long Truelove had to leave with her or else give away the fact that she was doing a little fishing on the sly. So she just walked her on back to the house, dragging the cow with her, and leaving her hook anchored in the pond. When she got back the next day she found a perch dangling on it that was so big it lasted four suppers. Every time she'd think about how she grabbed that fish off that hook, wrapped it in her newspaper, stuck it in her skirt under her smock and made it back home fast as she could, she'd laugh herself into the ground. The laughing cracked her side when she remembered her quick story to Old Lady Thompson about leaving so fast because she'd had a sign and thought the baby was coming before its time.

As Truelove got closer and closer to getting down, the chore of tugging the cow up the road to the highway and all the way to the pond became almost impossible. Often she was seen being dragged by the cow instead of the other way around. The cow had become so accustomed to being taken day in and day out up by the pond that it knew the route well enough to have gone by itself. When Truelove untied it from the post, it took off in a trot, almost running, making it difficult for her to keep hold of the rope. Truelove often thought of letting it go by itself but she was afraid that someone would steal it. Besides needing the fish she was smuggling out of the pond, she needed the cow even more for the milk it would provide for the baby. So she just resigned herself to trotting back and forth with it.

The cow never stopped getting on her nerves and she never stopped hating Henry's mother for giving it to them. Even though she saw it as some kind of curse, she was determined not to let it beat her down. So she tried all she could to make things easier for herself. Every day before she left the house she'd fill her pockets full of rocks and whenever the cow would stop along the road or anywhere, she'd just take a rock and plunk the cow in the rear end and it would take off with a start.

When fall came and the green grass was all parched and brown and Truelove's garden had long ago yielded its last bean, Henry erected a makeshift barn on the garden plot. Now the cow spent all of its time in the barn awaiting the birth of its calf and Truelove was left with little to do during the day. So she took up sewing and handstitched all kinds of little white dresses and jackets for the baby.

The cow had her calf about a month or so before Truelove had her baby. So by the time the baby arrived, the cow's milk was good and drinkable. Even though the cow seemed to give it reluctantly, there was plenty of fresh milk for the calf and for Truelove and all the troubles the cow had caused her gradually began to fade into the past. And for the first six months after the baby was born, Truelove was happy—happy that the baby had finally come, that the milk was coming good, that the cow was happy with its calf, and most of all that Henry was happier than she'd ever seen him. He had to leave for work around five so he was up and gone long before Truelove and the baby awoke in the morning. But when he returned, he'd take a bath, eat his supper and spend the rest of the evening with the baby. Truelove had never seen him softer than when he sat in that old squeaky rocker singing the baby to sleep.

> *Goooo to sle-eepy, Daddy's ba-aaby,*
> *Goooo to sle-eepy, Daddy's ba-aaby,*
> *Mama's gone away*
> *Papa's gone to stay*
> *Left nobo-ody but the ba-aaby*
> *Go to sle-eepy, Daddy's ba-aaby . . .*

39

Truelove hated when he sang that song. Whenever he did she was reminded of all the little black
babies running around in the quarters without a
daddy. More than that, she was disturbed by a
sense of doom in Henry every time he'd sing it. He
had a minor accident on the job one day and when
he came home he was in some mood. That night
he sang that song over and over and over. Even
after the baby was asleep and he'd put her in bed,
he sat rocking and singing. Sometimes she could
actually see him thinking that he was not good
enough to be a father, and that his trying to raise a
family on the fifty dollars a week he earned at the
sawmill was absurd.

That mood of his depressed Truelove for days.
But then there were nights when he'd come home,
after having a fairly good day at the sawmill,
laughing and joking. On those nights he'd sing
"Oh Mah Baby, Mah Curly-Headed Baby." Listening to him then, Truelove wished she had fifteen
babies so she could hear him singing to them all
night long.

As the baby neared a year and started to walk,
Truelove began to notice funny little movements
and gestures that bugged her. At first she was
slightly worried that something might be wrong
with the baby, but as she grew and grew and began
to walk, run and talk, Truelove came to see as

clear as day that little Louella was marked. She now recognized that all those strange motions she'd been observing for months were not those of a child but of a cow. Not only did she see that the baby held her head kind of cocked to one side when she was listening, and slightly nodded it back and forth when she talked, but that her eyes were overlarge and bulgy like a cow's. And the older little Louella got the more she resembled the cow.

One day Truelove got up enough nerves to tell Henry that she thought she'd marked the baby by always being around the cow when she was pregnant. She asked him if he thought the baby resembled a cow. He laughed and told her she was crazy and that the cow was still too much on her brains and that the baby didn't look like anybody but him. His reply somewhat reassured her and after that she tried to look at Louella without thinking about the cow, but hard as she tried she just couldn't help seeing that damn cow.

Even though little Louella was supersensitive and extremely bright, because she slightly resembled a cow—and it wasn't so much the resemblance as the air of cowness about her—everybody began to treat her as though she was dumb. Truelove first, then gradually Henry, then all of Truelove's friends and everyone else who came to the house. Same as the cow was always doing things to annoy and embarrass Truelove, the older Louella got the more she began to do the same. Truelove had a habit of talking at the child. She spat out all of her inner feelings about people she knew and things she'd done, and things she was going to do, as if Louella didn't exist. So at the age of four Louella was like a little old woman. Often, in the presence of company, she'd blurt out something Truelove had said, never exactly as Truelove had meant it, but with her own little put-downs packed in. Truelove began to see her as just as much of a burden as the cow had been and finally concluded that Henry's mother had truly cursed her.

"Good evenin, Miss Lily, you sho looks good in dat white dress," little five-year-old Louella was saying. "Mama's a always talkin bout how nice and white you is wit yo white house, yo white car an yous white dresses—dat you's just like dem white lilies in dat garden."

"Why, Louella," Lily was saying, "all lilies ain't white. Ain't yo mama never told you bout yellow lilies? Why, there's even a bright-red lily."

"Yeah, but Mama say you's a white one."

Truelove had been in the garden when she first heard Louella talking to Lily but now she stood at the front gate with her sun hat on and hoe in hand watching Louella and Lily walking towards her.

She was furious at Louella. Just the day before Truelove had been talking with Henry about how she couldn't stand Lily and all her pretentious ways.

"Look at yo hands! Git in that house and wash em!" she yelled, giving Louella a hard slap on her buttocks as she passed. "You on yo way to the store?" she said to Lily as she came up to her. "Ah jus run out of salt. Ah'll git some money and you could bring me a box if you don't mind."

"Why, you know I ain't walkin all the way up to dat store. I just saw you out in the garden an thought I'd come down and say hello but I'll go back home and git you a little salt if you needs it— but I don't know if I should since Louella told me what you said bout my white house and white car and white clothes."

"Dat gal always talkin somethin she ain't knows what she's talkin bout," Truelove said defensively.

"That child just repeatin what she done heard. I know all you niggers talk bout me behind my back but it makes me no difference cause I know you's just jealous. I'll be right back wit that salt."

Truelove stood there in the road looking at Lily's back walking away from her. "Look at that! Twenty-three years old and dressed like a little girl," she thought. "*Sure* you just dropped down to say hello all right. Mighty funny you done started dropping by every other day just bout the time Henry gits off work."

Lily lived up on the hill from Truelove and Henry. Her husband was killed three years ago on the job and Lily received several thousand dollars in insurance. She used the money to remodel her house. She had it painted snow-white, bought herself a snow-white Chevrolet, a bunch of white outfits, and ran around with white men as she'd never done before. Aside from that, now that her old man was dead, just about every nigger in the quarters was after her. But Lily, with her hard-to-get self, wasn't interested in the ones who were after her but only in the ones who weren't. So far Henry hadn't paid her any attention. But Truelove knew as she stood there watching Lily switching her ass down the road in front of her that she was on Henry's tail and she'd better put a stop to it before anything got started.

When Henry was eating his supper that same evening, Louella jumped up on his lap and shouted, "Daddy, that inshunce man tol Mama dat he sho did like her. Then he give Mama a big kiss right on the mouth." Henry jumped straight up from the table, dropping little Louella on the floor.

"What's this heah talk bout that damn insurance man? Buddy told me he was worse than a snake in the grass. Um gonna go up there and tell that nig-

44

ger if he ever sets foot in this house again I'll kill him."

Truelove was so scared she almost jumped out of her skin. She tried to tell Henry that she'd told the man not to come back to the house, that she'd go into town and pay at the agency from then on. But the whole time she was talking Henry was shouting so loud she couldn't even hear herself and she was sure he hadn't even heard a word. He left his supper on the table, put on his coat and jumped in that old pickup truck and left.

Soon as he was out of the door, Louella caught another spanking. That was her second one in less than two hours. Then three days later she got another one for something else she'd done. And they came regularly from then on.

The more Truelove beat Louella the more stubborn the child got. Truelove would tell her something to do and she'd act as though she didn't even hear her. Sometimes Truelove'd go right up to her and shout demands into her ear. But Louella'd simply turn her head and coolly look Truelove straight in the eyes. If she saw that Truelove was on the verge of spanking her she'd stop whatever she was doing and do what Truelove wanted of her. Often though, depending on how she felt, she refused to do what Truelove asked and took the spanking. But whether she did it or not, she always managed to convey to Truelove that she was doing it against her will and that Truelove was just as much of a pain in the ass as herself.

Things got so bad between Truelove and Louella that Henry was forced to intervene. He told Truelove to let up on Louella, that it wasn't Louella's fault that she was the way she was, that Truelove should let the child go and play with the other kids in the quarters whether she got along with their mamas or not.

At first, Truelove took Henry's advice all wrong. She reacted as though he'd put her down, as if he'd indirectly called her a bad mother. For days she was hurt and angry. Within time the mood passed and she finally conceded that Louella did need friends her own age, so, for the first time in the five and a half years Truelove had lived there, she visited some of the mothers up in the quarters. She explained little Louella's situation and got permission for her to play a few hours a day with their kids. That arrangement didn't last very long. Every day, within thirty minutes or so after Louella had been left with the other children, she was dragged back home screaming and kicking, and Truelove was told by whoever returned her that Louella was impossible, that she just didn't get along with the rest of the children.

In a deep depression and on the brink of a nervous breakdown, Truelove went to the doctor only to discover she was pregnant again. With this news she went home, fell flat on her face and hardly got out of bed for a week. Now, same as when she was pregnant with Louella, she took up her rocking and spent most of the day on the porch in the old squeaky rocker, thinking about her life and wondering whether it was fate or just her stupidity that had landed her there in that bottom of sand.

She resigned herself to everything, to the cow she hated, the child she couldn't manage, to Henry —her dear, sweet Henry—who out of his exasperation with her and the demeaning job at the sawmill had fallen into an affair with Lily.

While Truelove sat there rocking and waving to passers-by, Louella played in the sandy angle by the fork in the road. It was dangerous for the child to play there. But whenever Truelove saw or heard a car coming she'd yell to Louella to get back if she was too near the road. Since Truelove was worrying most of the time she was rocking, she sometimes noticed a car only after it was well past the house.

Usually when Louella played out in the yard, the cow was there too; same as Louella, it had no place else to go. One day just as a speeding car neared the curve, the cow suddenly stepped out right in front of it. The young driver swerved to avoid hitting the cow and crushed Louella into the sand, killing her instantly. As he passed the porch he shouted to Truelove, "You'd better keep that damn cow out of the road," indicating that he wasn't aware that he'd just run over the child.

Truelove, numb and speechless, just sat there staring at Louella stretched out in the sand. By the time she pulled herself together the car was well on its way. But it didn't matter. She knew the boy who did it. In a daze she slowly got up out of the chair, with her big belly wobbling in front of her, walked into the house, took the shotgun down off the wall, walked back outside, went shakily down the steps right past the dead child straight up to the cow, aimed the shotgun right at its head and blew its brains out. Then she picked Louella up in her arms, hoisting the child over her big belly and across one shoulder.

She slowly walked back to the porch, laid the dead child down on it, then sat down in her rocker and resumed her rocking. Through the tears streaming down her cheeks, Truelove looked at Louella. She saw for the first time that Louella's hair was parted straight down the middle and braided in two big plaits turned towards each other, like horns—cow horns. She didn't remember plaiting the child's hair like that. She hardly even remembered ever thinking of the child looking like a cow. But instinctively she got down on her knees, took the dead child's plaits loose, pulled her hair back in a ponytail, closed her bulgy cowlike eyes, and began rearranging her clothes.

Bobo

A little girl was under a pear tree. She was stealing pears, great big pears that had fallen all over the ground among the colorful leaves. She had a radio and her dog with her.

She was in a very mischievous mood. That morning she had felt depressed and whenever she got depressed it always ended in her doing something mischievous. Today she decided to defy her parents' order never to leave the house. She hated that house. She'd always hated it and yearned to be happy and in a beautiful place, to enjoy the sun just like she was enjoying it now. How she wanted to get away from that house and the cold winter that was coming. She hated all those little shacks she passed along the road with the slatted wood porches and the little stovepipes sticking out from the side of the house. She hated her house more than all of those she passed walking there on the road.

She hated it because it was very cold and had big cracks in it, and in the winter they had to stuff up the cracks with rags and newspapers that got wet with rain and smelled. She hated that little ugly potbellied heater that looked like a little squatted-down glowing monster from her bed at night, that did not give off any heat, that did not give off nothing.

Most of all she hated the house because she was always there by herself. Her parents said she was too young to be in the fields, but she knew it wasn't at all because she was too young. They didn't want her in the fields because she was puny. They said she was a sickly little girl and should be taken care of and that the sun was no good for her. But oh, how she loved the sun! She loved all the things they said were no good for her. Other children loved the sun and all and were allowed to enjoy them. Why couldn't she? She didn't want to be different and today she wouldn't be different. Today she would be just like all the other children.

Sometimes she would sneak to the edge of their neighbors' field and watch their children going back and forth carrying water to the adults. They looked so happy. If she were only allowed to carry water or bring her parents empty croker sacks when they needed them like all the other children did. But since she couldn't do that she would do what she imagined other children did. She would go for a walk with her dog. After all, when her brother gave her the dog he said, "This dog will keep you company and protect you. It'll be like your friend when Mama them's down there in the field. You can go for walks with it and you can play with it just like you'd play with a friend."

Yes, this day she would go for a walk with Bobo in spite of her mother's warning never to leave home, only to go around the fields where they could see her. But she didn't want to walk around the fields. She didn't always want to be where they could see her. She was just tired of walking around the fields and sitting on the porch and hating that house.

She took her radio and Bobo and headed up the rock road, walking slowly and cautiously as if someone might yell after her. Once she was some distance away from the house she began to breathe more freely, and the farther away she got the more daring she felt. She skipped, she sang, she teased the dog, she tossed rocks at trees, and she ran faster than she was ever allowed around the house.

When she tired and began walking more slowly she saw things as she had never seen them before. She had never really looked at the trees—she didn't know there were so many different kinds of leaves. Even this road she had ridden over many times in the car on the way to school or going shopping with her mother or going to church, seemed entirely different now that she was really on it.

She saw the tree full of fruit through a fence in a pasture near the road. She couldn't tell what kind of tree it was from that distance but she could see that it was hanging with fruit. She felt like running in and taking some but she was afraid, so she walked on a little ways, thinking how much she would like some of whatever fruit it was. Then her mood of daring came surging back and she quickly darted through the fence and ran towards the tree, Bobo at her side. Coming up under it she saw that it was full of pears. She sat her radio down among the leaves on the ground and hastily began gathering up an armful of pears. Suddenly she stopped and mused to herself:

"Why am I scrappin them up and runnin like I'm scared? I'm just gonna put all these down and test em. Who knows, these on the ground may not be any good. They may be half rotten, so I'll have to climb the tree to get some fresher ones." The idea of climbing the tree appealed to her immensely.

Once she had carefully put all the pears down on the ground again, she made an attempt to climb the tree. There was only one lower limb and even it was too high for her to get a good grasp on it. She had never climbed a tree before and her failure to do so now brought back her feeling of being weak and helpless.

She returned to the pears she had piled up on the ground and sat down beside them. Looking up at the juicy pears hanging from the tree she reluctantly picked one off her pile and began eating it. Sure enough, just as she thought, it was a little overripe. But it was sweet, tangy and good. She held it up before her face with her head slightly tilted back, letting the juice drip on her tongue. It tasted like honey dripping down.

She reached over and turned up the music on the radio, then patted the bare ground for Bobo to come and sit beside her. Recognizing the sound of the cello, as her brother had called it, she remembered that he had promised to bring her some "classical records" on his next trip from California. She wished that her mother liked the cello and then maybe she would buy some classical records instead of gospel. Then she could play them any time she got ready. She wouldn't have to sit and listen for it to come on the radio.

She stroked the back of Bobo's head. Once her

brother brought the records maybe her mother would let her play them on the box since she never let anybody outside of herself touch that box. She said it cost too much money and she didn't want anyone "tamperin wit it." Anyway she had seen how her mother worked the box and maybe she would sneak and play her cello records when her mother them were in the fields. The thought of sneaking reminded her that she was sneaking now and that if her mother came back to the house for something and found her gone she would certainly get her rump whipped.

"Gal, if you leave this house I'll tan your hide."

Listening to the warm enveloping sound of the cello and feeling the hot pull of the sun, she felt herself slowly slipping away, enwrapped in happiness. It was such a beautiful fall day with the sun crisping on the leaves, it brought out their colors like she had never seen them before, all the beautiful reds and yellows and browns. The sun seemed to be flooding everything, filling up the whole pasture, drowning everything with light. She thought of her parents and she could see them gathering corn and laughing.

When the music stopped she began raking the pile of pears into her skirt but it struck her that if she took them back to the house it would give away the fact that she had been out. So she scattered the pears back out among the leaves, thinking that she and Bobo would come back again, every day if possible, and listen to the beautiful music and just enjoy how beautiful it was there. But she felt guilty, guilty that she couldn't take any of the pears back and share them with the others. Then it came to her as she was thinking about all that beauty and coming back to take the pears every day, that they would not always be there. Soon they would have fallen off the tree and would all be rotten, and even tomorrow it might be rainy and ugly and cold and she would have to stay in the house all day.

The thought of being in that wet smelly house made her feel choked and sad. Often when she was alone she would dance, just dance to the classical music, stretch her arms and whirl and turn until she felt better. Now as the music began again she turned it up loud and just let it flow all the way through her, just like the sun going in and out of all of her. She danced among the pears on the ground, going around them and crushing the crackling leaves and kicking them up with her toes. The music blaring, sun shining, as she danced around the tree, picking up leaves, arms full of leaves, throwing them over her head, dancing all over the tree, everywhere, and the dog was just sitting there wagging his tail and looking at her.

"Oh, come on, Bobo, be happy, dance with me, Bobo."

She took a big pile of leaves and threw them over the dog's head trying to get him to be happy with her but he didn't even move, he just let the leaves fall all over him. He wanted to play and he didn't want to play. He lapped his tongue at her lovingly. She smiled and took another pile of leaves and threw them over him. This time as the leaves began falling over him Bobo stood up and began wagging his tail and shaking his head from side to side.

Oh, Bo-bo, won't you dance with me . . .
Look, Bo-bo, look at me dance!
It feels soooo good to dance, to stre-etch . . .

And all around him the leaves were falling. . . .

Oh, Bo-bo, let's be happy,
Dance, Bobo!
Dance, Bobo!
Look at me dance, Bobo. . . .

She kept dancing and kicking up leaves until Bobo grew tired and quit looking. Then she stopped for a moment and looked at the sun, overcome by a feeling of gratitude. Slowly she began to dance again, this time stretching and bowing to the sun, as if to pay tribute and offer thanks for such a beautiful day. As she danced she felt the sun was watching, beaming down on her and the whole scene with pleasure.

Suddenly a voice said out of the woods, right next to the pear tree, very gruff and deep:

WHAT ARE YOU DOIN OVER HERE STEAL-IN THESE PEARS! YOU HAVE NO BIDNESS ON THIS PROPERTY!

All of a sudden she was standing there. She had completely lost her bearings.

DIDN'T YOU HEAR ME? WHAT ARE YOU DOIN ON THIS HERE PROPERTY!

Now she began to run very fast, leaving the radio and Bobo behind. She didn't even know in which direction she ran. Her heart was hurting so, it filled up her whole chest, her mouth and even her ears. When she looked back she could see Bobo guarding the radio and barking up a storm but she couldn't hear a thing because her ears were filled up with the pounding of her heart.

"*Run*, Bobo, *run*, Bobo!"

She knew she was saying it but she couldn't even hear her own voice. Bobo didn't move but she kept on running, looking back over her shoulder and screaming at what she thought was the top of her voice.

Once she got outside the fence she turned and

looked back. Bobo was still under the tree barking and looking towards the woods as if he was about to spring to attack.

Her brother had warned her when he had given her Bobo as a puppy that German shepherds could be vicious, and never to provoke him once he grew up because he might even turn on her if he were angry enough. She had never seen Bobo as angry as he was now and she was afraid for the man in the woods who had yelled at her.

She crouched down by the fence and started calling Bobo again. She was too far away for him to hear her, but she kept screaming and calling anyway.

She saw a little white boy run towards Bobo. When she saw the boy she knew it wasn't him that made the voice. It must have been a man—his father, she figured. There could have been more people in the woods because now she remembered, when the voice yelled out, she had heard someone laughing. She expected to see the boy's father come out of the woods after him but nobody followed. Bobo was barking and barking. She knew he would attack the boy if he got any closer. She wondered why the father didn't come out of the woods and stop the boy. As the boy began to move past Bobo towards the radio, she began screaming again.

"Bobo, calm down! Calm down, Bobo!"

Suddenly the boy snatched the radio and started back towards the woods. But before he could leave Bobo jumped on him. He leaped up taller than the boy and landed on his neck, bringing him down. She was sure Bobo would kill him. As the boy slumped down on the ground, she fainted.

When she woke up, the boy had disappeared. She knew Bobo had killed him but she still hoped that the boy's father had finally come out of the woods and beat Bobo off the boy. Maybe he wasn't killed, maybe he took the boy back to their house. And if he was hurt badly, maybe his father took him to the hospital.

Anyway, whatever had happened, the boy was gone, but Bobo was still there. The radio was turned over in the leaves and Bobo stood over it, panting heavily, still guarding it. She wanted to go back and get Bobo and the radio but she was too scared. She remembered her brother's warning and for the first time she was afraid of Bobo. She figured that he wouldn't hurt her but she didn't want to take any chances. He stood there with his long tongue lapping out, looking cruel and mean, as if he would destroy anything that came near him.

She didn't know what to do, so she just sat there on the edge of the road hidden in the bushes watching him. She wanted to call Bobo but he was too far away. Anyway she was too scared to call him. She was too scared to do anything for fear of Bobo and the people who might be waiting there in the woods in case she came back, so they could get her. Otherwise, she wondered, why would they leave Bobo and the radio and the boy was gone?

She was also scared to go back home. She didn't know how long she had been lying there faint. It must have been a long time for it was now twilight, past time for her mother them to come home from the fields. She couldn't bring herself to leave Bobo and the radio so she stayed and stayed until it grew completely dark and she couldn't see them anymore. She knew that by now her parents were looking for her, and if she stayed in that spot, which was not too far from their house, they would find her there. She thought for some time, then remembered that there was a place in the woods even closer to their house where she could hide. Nobody knew about it. It was all covered over by vines like a little cave. She and Bobo had discovered it one day they played there, and ever since they had used it as their little secret house. The vines were so thick that even when it rained they didn't get wet.

She decided to go and spend the night there. Then she would get up early the next morning and run away.

So she headed back along the road, walking as close to the woods as possible. Whenever there was a car or she heard the slightest noise she dove into the bushes until it had passed. It was late now and most of the shacks she went by were dark, with only an occasional dim light burning here and there. When she neared her own house, she crawled under the fence on the property across the road and continued walking until she came directly in front of her house. Then she stopped and peered through the bushes. The porch light was on but the rest of the house was completely dark. She knew that her mother them were out looking for her. She thought that her mother must be half crazy with worry. She was tempted to go inside and wait until they came and tell them everything.

She paused there for a long time but she just couldn't bring herself to do it, so she went on to her little viny cave.

When she got there she crawled in and lay down on the leaves. She was so tired she couldn't think about anything. Everything that had happened during the day blurred into one big mass, blotting out everything. So she curled up among the leaves and fell asleep.

She awoke unable to stop thinking about the boy. Was he in the hospital? Had the father or somebody just taken him up in their arms and carried him to the hospital or home somewhere? She could see them in the hospital with the boy lying there almost dead, and the parents worried and crying.

All heavy-hearted, not knowing what to do, she lay there under the vines, crying, thinking about Bobo, the radio, the boy, and whether he would die.

After a while she could hear her mother them out on the edge of the woods. They were calling her, so many people were calling her, all in the woods. They were right near and all around her. She started praying that they wouldn't find her. They came very close and she held herself absolutely still, without even breathing. Then she could hear her mother's voice very loud and clear as if she was standing right over her.

"She's not in these here woods, I tol you, I tol you, somebody done come here and took that gal! Where was that damn dog? They done took the dog too!"

"That dog coulda done *hurt* her or somethin," she heard her father say. "That's a vicious-ass dog! She could be layin here in these woods, half-dead or sometin. I tol you we shoulda got ridda that damn dog."

"Bobo wouldn't hurt Lily-Mae. Shoot, that dog grew *up* wit that gal, wasn't nothin but a puppy when Buddy brought him here. That gal'd be the last person in the worl that dog would hurt! You see how he play wit her. . . ."

"You can never tell bout them damn dogs. They'll play, but the first thing done outta line they'll turn on you. She coulda done did sometin to make him mad."

"Sheriff Riley, ain't no needa us stayin out here lookin all night. She ain't here. I jus *know* somebody done took her. T'morrow I want you to such this whole *town* for her. Ah'm goin to be up to yo office bright and early. I want you to go out there wit me to Bill Hackett's place so we can look aroun. I tol you . . ." she heard her mother's voice fading out as she walked away, "I tol you he keeps pesterin me bout buyin that damn dog. . . ."

Now that they were gone she began to breathe again. It was very quiet, quiet enough for her to hear the slight breeze rustling the dry leaves hanging from the trees. She lay calmly for a while, feeling safe. When they left in the morning to go out to Bill Hackett's, she would run away.

Now she thought of Bobo again. What if Bill Hackett came by and saw Bobo on the road or under the pear tree? He would certainly take him and nobody would never know. She remembered Bill Hackett had offered her mother fifty dollars for Bobo, but her mother had said, "This dog ain't for sale. Buddy brought that dog all the way from

California for Lily-Mae's Christmas present. That gal'd have a *fit* if I sell this dog! Sides, we need him for a watchdog too."

When her mother had said they needed it for a watchdog, Hackett asked her, looking around at their shack, "What you have here worth watchin?"

When Hackett left, her father got angry and cursed and called him all kinds of names.

"My chile got just as much right to have a watchdog as them white chaps o his."

Once again she felt like going in and telling her mother everything that had happened, but something still held her back.

Finally she fell asleep. When she woke up the next morning and emerged from her viny den she found the sun high in the sky and very bright. "I gotta get away from this close to the house," she thought, "cause when they don't find me or Bobo at Bill Hackett's or anywhere else, they'll come and search these woods again." She sneaked away, out from the woods, stooping down and looking about her as she went. When she came to the road she darted across it and went way over through the woods. She knew there were some empty old shacks over there. She remembered seeing them on one of the many walks she and Buddy took when he was home. She was sure that by now they had already searched the shacks and seen that she wasn't there and that they wouldn't look there again. She could stay in one of the shacks until it was dark. By then she hoped she would have figured out what to do.

It took her some time to figure out which shack was safest. They were all rottening down with the doors hanging off the hinges and all the windows broken. They looked as if hadn't anyone lived in them for a long time. There were seven or eight of them grouped together like it had once been a little community. Her brother told her that the people who once lived there had all been plantation hands and that they moved away when the foreman of the plantation killed one of the workers. She did not know which house the murdered worker had lived in and she hoped she wouldn't pick his house to hide in.

Finally she decided on the one farthest back and nearest to the woods. That way if she heard anyone coming she could run out and hide in the woods again.

Once she was inside the shack she saw that it was much larger than it looked from the outside. There were two big rooms with very low ceilings. Cobwebs were strung from wall to wall in the large room with the fireplace. It was completely empty except for some old rusty tin plates lying on the floor. In the second room there was an old wood stove leaning against the back wall on three legs and a broken-down kitchen cabinet sitting in the middle of the floor. It looked like all kinds of animals and birds used the place—there were bird shit and rabbit turds everywhere she stepped. The damp musty animal stench nauseated her and she was about to leave for another shack when she looked up and noticed that there was a trap door in the ceiling above the old cabinet. It looked as if someone had used the cabinet to climb up in the loft. She was hesitant about staying there, but curious to see what was up there anyway, so she climbed up on the cabinet and unlatched the trap door. It flapped down and hit the ceiling with a loud bang, startling her. She peeped in and saw that it was tiny and dark, and extremely sooty. Now that she was up on the cabinet, getting down seemed like too much trouble to her, so she climbed in. She crawled into one of the dark corners underneath the slanted roof and sat there in all that soot. She was very miserable but the closeness of it made her feel safe.

It was very dark but once on the floor she saw a long split in the ceiling through which a sliver of sunlight shone. She followed the ray of light to the opposite wall and saw that it was focused right on a big cobweb. She didn't see the spider but a few dead flies were securely entwined there.

After sitting uncomfortably for what she thought to be a few hours, she saw the spider return to its web. It was such a huge ugly thing it frightened her. She jumped right up and quickly climbed down out of the loft, thinking that there might be other spiders there in the darkness that she couldn't see.

Now that she was down she saw that it was dusk and that within an hour or so it would be dark and she could run away. If she had to run away at night she'd better go get Bobo. The shacks weren't too far from the pear tree where she'd left Bobo and the radio. Even though it was just the day before that she'd left him, it seemed as though she hadn't seen him in a long time. She was anxious to go and see if he was still there.

Just before it was completely dark she left the shack, cut through the woods and headed in the direction of the pear tree. Within a short time she had come to the clearing where the pear tree was, and she felt proud of herself for having come right to it. Her spirits were immediately dampened when she didn't see Bobo. Had something happened to him? Maybe her mother them found him while they were looking for her and had taken him home. And again she felt like going to the house and confessing everything but still she could not draw herself to do it. So she sat there on the edge of the woods and cried a long time about Bobo. She cried and cried. While sitting there crying, a white girl about her age came up to her from the woods behind, startling her. She jumped straight up, shaking.

After a while the white girl said, "I'm scared too."

She looked at her and didn't say anything but wondered what she had to be scared of. Her thought must have shown on her face because the white girl started explaining.

"Your dog *killed* my brother," she said in a tearfully broken voice. "I watched your dog kill my brother. Then he . . . he . . . he . . . he ate him up."

"Bobo ate him up?"

"He ate him up. I was so frightened. I'm *still* scared, too scared to go home."

"Bobo ate him up? Bobo ate him up? I can't believe it, I can't believe it, I absolutely can't believe Bobo would eat up a person, I can't believe that, you're telling me a *story*, you're telling me a story, Bobo wouldn't eat anybody. Bobo wouldn't eat *any*body—Bobo didn't eat him, because the boy's father was in the woods. I *know* the boy's father was in the woods—he *yelled* at me. He wouldn't let Bobo eat his boy. Stop telling me stories!"

But as she stood there looking at her, she knew the girl wasn't telling a lie.

"What did your father do?"

And the white girl said:

"It wasn't my father in the woods. It was just me and Johnny-Joe. It was Johnny-Joe who yelled at you. I told him not to but he did anyway. I *knew* he would scare you. I didn't want him to scare you, cause I wanted to keep watchin you dance. You dance *so* pretty."

When the white girl mentioned her dancing and all, Lily-Mae said:

"It was *you* in the woods with him?"

"Yes, there was just me and Johnny-Joe."

"What is your family sayin? Did they kill Bobo? Where is Bobo?"

"No, they didn't kill Bobo. They don't even know Johnny-Joe is dead. They're probably lookin for us everywhere. I'm afraid to go home and tell them. I can't go home."

"I can't go home either. I slept in the woods under some vines all night. . . . Did you see what happened to Bobo?"

"No, I was so afraid, I ran away and hid in another part of the woods. I was afraid he would find me and eat me too." When the white girl said that, she started crying and crying again.

"I can't believe that about Bobo, Bobo eatin people, Bobo killin people. . . ." Finally she asked, "What are you goin to do now?"

She asked the white girl the question since *she* hadn't figured out what to do, as if she was asking *herself* the question, like "what are we *both* going to do?"

The white girl answered:

"I don't know, I'm just so scared."

And Lily-Mae said:

"I tell you what, you come and stay in the shack with me tonight, and maybe we can figure out something to do."

"Johnny-Joe had no bidness yelling at you. It was *his* fault and don't you feel bad, your dog wouldn't have attacked him had he not taken your radio."

Lily-Mae started crying again and the white girl started crying too. They stood there together, crying and hugging.

Finally she said:

"It's dark now, we better go back to the shacks. You come and stay with me in my shack."

"No, mine is much better than yours. I know which one you're in and mine is so much better. I've made a bed of shucks and it's very roomy."

"Are you stayin in one of those shacks too?"

"Yes."

And all the way to the shack Lily-Mae kept thinking, "The same thing, we went through the same thing. . . ."

When they arrived at the shack Lily-Mae saw that it wasn't really a shack but an old barn with lots of hay and shucks stacked around the sides of the walls. It was immense, with big wide steps leading to a second tier like a balcony, and she thought that if anyone came they never would find them under all that hay. They both carried enough hay up into the balcony to make a bed for Lily-Mae.

The white girl had taken some of the pears from the tree and had them stacked on the floor near her shuck bed. The sight of those pears reminded Lily-Mae that she had not eaten in almost two days. She just dove over and took one without even asking. They were sitting up there talking and eating pears when all of a sudden they heard a dog bark outside.

"Oh, that's Bobo, that's Bobo, I know it's Bobo!" Lily-Mae shouted, completely forgetting that Bobo had gone mad and killed a boy. She started running down the steps to get him.

"Don't go down, don't go down, he'll kill you, *please* don't go down!"

"Bobo is my friend, Bobo won't hurt me, Bobo *loves* me."

She opened the big swinging doors. Her heart leaped in her throat when she saw Bobo standing there in the twilight. She just fell down on her knees and started hugging him. Bobo licked her and she cried and cried.

"Oh Bobo, you are *bad*. You killed a boy. Why

would you kill somebody, Bobo? What's happening to you?" All the time she was crying and hugging him.

She brought him inside the barn with her and closed the big doors behind them. When she started walking up the stairs Bobo began barking and making up a lot of noise, showing how glad he was to see her.

"Shh! Shh! Shh!" she said, trying to make him be quiet. When he continued, she yelled, "You'll make somebody find us, be quiet!" Bobo quieted now and started walking up the stairs beside her. Just as she reached the top, he started barking again. She turned around to yell at him and scratched her arm on a rusty nail sticking out of the banister.

"Oh, I cut myself," she said, heading towards the white girl. She saw that the white girl was sitting covered up to her head with hay, and the hay was shaking all over.

"Don't bring him in here! Don't bring him in here! He'll *kill* us, he'll kill us! Oh please, pleee-ease don't bring him in here."

"Oh no, he won't hurt us," Lily-Mae said. "See, he's so glad to see me."

When she said that, she turned around to hug Bobo to show that he wouldn't hurt them. She put her arms around Bobo's neck to hug and stroke him, trying to make the white girl feel at ease.

76

"See, he will go away with us," she said, stroking his head. "He will protect us. He won't let anybody hurt us."

As she stroked his head, a little blood dripped from the wound but she did not seem to notice it. Bobo smelled the blood and started licking it.

"Stop it, Bobo! What's wrong with you . . . stop it!" she yelled. Instead of stopping, he started licking much faster, going all the way from her wrist towards the gash in her arm.

"Stop it, Bobo, stop it!" she screamed with terror. The white girl covered her head completely and disappeared under the shucks.

"Oh, Bobo, Bobo, no no no, Bobo! *No*, Bobo!" she screamed as he slashed into her arm with his teeth.

"Bobo! Bobo!" she continued to yell as she hit him in the head with all of her might, but Bobo kept slashing at her, ripping the meat completely off her bone, eating her up. She continued screaming until she collapsed on the floor.

All Burnt Up

Lucille's mother died when she was five and her father remarried six months later to perhaps the meanest woman in the whole county. Her stepmother was a very ambitious person. She had three children of her own before marrying Lucille's father, whose dead wife had left him two. Saddled with five children and a mule, her stepmother set out to become a rich cotton queen. She forced Lucille to quit school when she was in the sixth grade to work in the cotton fields. Lucille hated farming more than she hated her stepmother so she ran away from home when she was only thirteen to stay with an aunt who lived in town. One day while her aunt was away, her aunt's brother came to the house and raped Lucille, leaving her pregnant. Her aunt, who'd once worked for a family named Hudson, got Lucille a job working for them when she was two months pregnant.

Lucille worked until she was five months before Old Lady Hudson realized that she was pregnant. She'd expected to be fired once it was known but she wasn't. Next to her own mother, who was dead, Old Lady Hudson turned out to be the nicest person she'd ever known. Not only was Lucille not fired, but she was given a house of her own. The following day when she returned to work, Old Lady Hudson spent the entire day in the old shack in back of her house with a handyman. After supper when Lucille was getting ready to leave, Old Lady Hudson thrust a key into her hand and said, "It's much too hot for you to be walking all the way from your aunt's here every day so I fixed up the shack out back. You can move in tomorrow."

Lucille was so happy she cried all the way home to her aunt's that evening. Then the next morning, with her aunt's blessing, she stuffed the few belongings she had into a pillow slip, threw them across her back, and walked the five miles to the Hudsons'.

Old Lady Hudson did everything she could to make things easy for Lucille. Before she moved into the shack she'd worked from breakfast to supper with only a thirty-minute break in between. Now she worked only two hours in the morning and was allowed to go to her little shack and rest during the heat of the day before returning to prepare supper.

Even though she was lonesome and missed her stepsisters and brother, she got used to living alone in the shack in no time. In the mornings when she got up she was usually sick and vomiting all over the place. Going to work was the last thing she felt like doing, but she went anyway. And when the two hours were up she'd return to the shack feeling a little better. First thing she'd do was take a nap, and then she'd spend the rest of the day lying up in bed reading magazines that Old Lady Hudson had given her.

One morning around five o'clock she woke up with cramps like she'd never had in her life. She knew the baby was on its way. Walking from her shack to the Hudsons' door she was afraid the baby would fall out on the ground. Immediately when Old Lady Hudson saw her standing there shaking with her belly vibrating like a drum, she knew they had to act quickly. So she walked Lucille back to her shack as fast as she could hop, put her in bed and summoned the next-door neighbor. When they returned to the shack Lucille had passed out and the baby's head had made its arrival.

When Lucille came to she saw Old Lady Hudson and her next-door neighbor sitting by her bed. Old Lady Hudson was holding a little bundle she handed to Lucille saying, "Here is your little poochie."

Old Lady Hudson treated Lucille just like her own fourteen-year-old daughter and practically took over the entire care of the baby. She took down one of the old cribs in her attic, cleaned it up, and put it up in the dining room for little Poochie. And then she watched her all day long while Lucille was doing her work. She even changed Poochie's diapers, picked her up and sang to her while she sucked her bottle, and told her funny little nonsense stories. She simply delighted in the child as if it were her very own.

All but one of Old Lady Hudson's four children were married and had children but they were all in their teens. None of the grandchildren lived in Mississippi. Her oldest child, a boy, lived in California; a girl, the next in line, was in Arkansas; and her other son with four children lived in Chicago. Old Lady Hudson saw them on the average of once a year, the grandchildren sometimes twice a year. Betsy, her youngest daughter, lived only twenty miles away in another small town. She'd only been married two years and was soon to have her first child. The Hudsons saw a lot of her. She and her husband would often come on Friday and spend the entire weekend.

Betsy was, in Old Lady Hudson's opinion, the worst of the children. Because she was so much younger than the older kids, she had been pampered and spoiled to death. Old Man Hudson, on the other hand, favored Betsy because she was the only one of the kids who stayed nearby and saw after them—in his opinion, the way children should when their parents are old and helpless. He was looking forward to the child she was soon to give birth to. Now at the age of sixty-two he found himself truly feeling like a man who was going to be a grandpa. The other grandchildren who'd all been born out of Mississippi, and whom he rarely saw, were virtual strangers to him. But with Betsy's kids things would be different. He'd see them all the time. In his eyes Betsy could do no wrong, even though she'd married and was going to have a baby for the son of one of the most racist rednecks in the state. Unlike Old Lady Hudson, who detested her son-in-law, Old Man Hudson constantly found himself making excuses for him whenever he made a racist remark or cracked a racist joke in Lucille's presence.

He was always making jokes about little Poochie crawling, running and playing around the Hudsons' house, and on many occasions wondered aloud about what kind of little nigger she was going to grow up to be.

Old Lady Hudson was so embarrassed for Lucille's sake she asked that Lucille not bring Poochie to the house when Betsy them were there. Since Lucille was off on Saturday and had only to prepare dinner on Sunday, she'd cook dinner while Poochie took her afternoon nap. In the evening she left for her two hours with an old Negro couple who lived down the road from the Hudsons while she served dinner and washed the dishes. Lucille resented having to part with Poochie for even two hours, but mostly she resented Old Lady Hudson for yielding to Betsy and her stupid-ass husband.

Then, two weeks later when Betsy's own newborn little Jill was occupying the crib in the Hudsons' dining room, Lucille concluded that, at root, Old Lady Hudson was just as much of a racist as Betsy. Every time she passed through the dining room and saw little Jill lying there in "Poochie's crib," with her lifeless little white hands and blood-red nose, she'd hiss at her and swear on a stack of Bibles that she was going to leave that prejudiced household. But of course, because she had nowhere else to go, she stayed on.

When Poochie was three, Mississippi had its worst winter in more than twenty-five years. It got extremely cold in November, and in December when it snowed, it was on the ground until March. Lucille and Poochie slept under six layers of blankets and quilts. But the thirty-year-old shack was made of only one thin layer of planks and wallpaper, and that winter, even though equipped with two heaters, it was as cold as if Lucille and Poochie had slept in a sleeping bag on the icy ground.

Around eleven o'clock one night when the temperature had dropped to about ten degrees, Old Lady Hudson, fearing that Lucille and Poochie would freeze to death, went out to the shack and brought them into her house, again endearing herself to Lucille. For now she'd once again been truly elevated from a maid to a member of the family. And she was so thankful she found herself cleaning the house at ten and eleven o'clock at night when everyone—Old Lady and Old Man Hudson and Poochie—was fast asleep. She'd sneak downstairs and dust all the furniture, take up spots on the living-room floor and rewax it, scrub down the refrigerator, stove and all the cabinets in the kitchen. Then when she'd tired herself out enough to sleep, she would sit for a while in Old Lady Hudson's big rocker near the fireplace and watch the red-hot logs dying out. During those moments the house was all her own and for the first time in her life she felt like "somebody."

Two weeks later though, when Betsy, her racist husband and their darling little Jill dropped in to spend the weekend, that feeling of being "somebody" for a change was shattered like a fragile piece of china hurled against a stone wall.

"I ain't never seen the likes of this in all my life!" Betsy stood screaming at the top of the stairs. "This is it!—this is the living end! And Mama, I ain't gonna stand for it! Either you make her take these damn"—she was running back and forth flinging Lucille and Poochie's clothes down the stairs one by one—"things back out in that shack this minute or I'm gonna leave this house and never set foot in it again!"

"But Betsy, honey," Old Lady Hudson pleaded. "It's too cold out there in that . . ."

"Don't you give me that stuff about it's too cold out there! I suppose you'd rather me and Bud and Jill sleep out there instead!"

Old Lady Hudson, Old Man Hudson, Bud and Lucille all stood at the bottom of the stairs looking up at Betsy there on the landing running back and forth, screaming like a crazy woman.

"I was only trying to do what is decent and proper, Betsy," Old Lady Hudson said feebly. "How could anyone in their right mind let a three . . ."

"What is *proper!*" Betsy shouted the word so

loud it hit the walls, fell apart letter by letter and shook the whole house before it bounced off. *"Proper* for where? Chicago—where Pete got your own flesh and blood up there sleeping, eating and camping out wit niggers? And then he's got the nerves to come back here to Mississippi and brag about it. I can see now you are mighty proud of him for it. Next thing I expect to hear from you is that Jill and Poochie can share a room.

"Look at this! I see now you have even been knitting clothes for that sweet little Poooooocccchiieee of yours," she said, flinging the little dress down the stairs smack into Lucille's face.

When she did that Lucille tore up the stairs after her, and Bud, seeing Lucille was angry enough to break every bone in Betsy's body, ran after Lucille. He caught her just at the top of the stairs. Lucille whirled, slinging him against the wall. As she went for his neck, he threw up both hands and pleaded:

"I ain't aiming to hurt you or nothing like that. I just think it's a bit unfair, you's bein so much bigger than mah wife."

"Don't you ever put yo filthy-ass hands on me again, you, you . . ." Lucille hissed right in his face. ". . . you damn peckerwood!" She turned and seeing Betsy running down the stairs in terror, shouted, "You stringy-haired little shit! I'm going in this room and get the rest of my things and then um leaving this damn house. If you be anywhere in mah sight when I comes out I might kill you. Miss Hudson, will you please git Poochie and git her ready for me?" she said and slammed into the room.

She was so nervous and shaky she sat on the bed for thirty minutes with her head in her hands crying herself out until she was satisfied with her resolute decision to leave that house for good. When she'd put the few things of hers into a pillow slip, she slowly made her way down the stairs. At the bottom, she found Old Lady Hudson standing there holding Poochie by the hand. She looked directly through the cataracts in Old Lady Hudson's eyes into the deepest depths of her soul and without one word passed between them, she took the clothes Betsy had thrown downstairs, which Old Lady Hudson had neatly folded in her arm, stuffed them into the pillow slip, and took Poochie by the hand and walked out of the house.

It was more than a year before Lucille broke her resolution to never set foot in the Hudsons' house again. Once she did she was always stopping by to see if Old Lady Hudson needed anything. Then just about every Saturday when she was off at the Fletchers' she'd take Poochie by the Hudsons' and insist on doing something around the house for her. Within a few weeks this routine became a regular part of Lucille's things to do on Saturday's list, and it went on like that for years.

"Hey Matt, throw me one!"

Matt let loose a fast one while Willy stood stiff with anticipation. The whole upper part of his body from his knees up was stiff while his legs from his knees down to the tips of his toes on which he stood twitched nervously. There was an intense, frightened excitement emanating from his eyes, his face—his whole being, even though his body conveyed so many other things.

One could hardly see the ball as it traveled from Matt's hand to Willy's glove, but within what seemed like seconds Willy was jumping up and down.

"Man, it's no question about it—you kin pitch, but shit, I kin catch too. Who knows, today it's Jackie Robinson, tomorrow it might just be me, Willy Tudor. Lay a couple a more right heah, baby," he said, throwing the ball back to Matt and socking his left hand into the mitt, making a loud muffled clapping noise.

The World Series had just begun and, in this tiny Southern town of 1300, just about every black boy beyond the age of five was determined to prove himself in baseball like Jackie Robinson had done.

The girls, well, they could always tell each other about the day when Johnny or Willy or Matt or one of the boys'd make it in baseball and would return to marry someone from home. Right now they were content with just being near the boys and having some of their excitement rub off on them.

Little Poochie was now eleven. She didn't have a father, a big brother, a favorite uncle or even a little brother onto whom she could project her baseball fantasy. She was even too young to be the girlfriend of any of the boys who made up the Little League team from around where she lived. Not only that, but she didn't even have a male teacher to dream about. She was in the sixth grade and all she'd ever had were women teachers. She couldn't remember a single dream she'd had about any of them and if she did they certainly weren't nice like the dreams a friend told her she had about Mr. Smith, the seventh-grade teacher. Well, next year she'd be in Mr. Smith's class and maybe she'd dream about him then. But next year, who knows, maybe she'd even have a boyfriend of her own to dream about.

As she stood there in the street with all the other boys and girls, watching Matt and Willy showing off, she thought maybe next year she'd be dreaming about Willy. He'd already shown her that he liked her. Why he even told her, one day last week, he was going to marry her when she grew up. Even though he was four years and three grades ahead of her, and even though she knew he was kidding, she believed him anyway. Yeah, she believed everything anybody ever told her—like Old Lady Hudson telling her that she was going to grow up and be a teacher like she'd been. Sure, she was going to grow up and be a teacher all right. And Old Lady Hudson was going to help her just like she said. She believed that even though Old Lady Hudson was sixty-nine years old and could hardly see.

"Ruby Lee! Gal, can't you walk faster than that?" she shouted at her little sister. "Mama's gonna be off work and if we ain't got that water by the time she gits home . . ."

Her little sister clutched her books and skipped ahead. Poochie realized now as she watched Ruby Lee bouncing in front of her that it was not Ruby Lee's fault that they were late—no, it was her own. Every single day this week she'd been late getting home. And every single day she'd blamed it on Ruby Lee when she was the one who was always fooling around watching Willy them clowning in the streets. Lately it seemed as though she was always watching Willy. Yeah, ever since last week when he said he was going to marry her she couldn't take her eyes off him. She looked back and saw the crowd still huddled around watching. She couldn't stand that aspect of Willy—he was always putting on a show for people and if he wasn't clowning or cutting up with a bunch of people surrounding him, he was sizing up to her and telling her stories about his intentions to marry her.

"Hey! Poochie!" She was now turning the curve to her house and it was Willy calling her. "Why you in such a rush today?" he shouted.

She bristled and stopped but then, deciding she was late enough as it was, ran around the curve straight up to the gate leading to her house. Little Ruby Lee had left it open for her and was now running up the gravelly path ahead of her. Once Poochie securely fastened the gate, she walked slowly up the path towards the house. When she was sure Willy'd turned the curve, she looked back. Sure enough, he had and was headed towards the gate as if he meant to come straight up to the house.

"What you running away for?" he said to her, somewhat angrily.

"I gotta get home before . . . before . . ." she began to say, then turned around to look at the house. Seeing her mother standing on the porch with the two water buckets in her hands, she walked quickly towards her.

"I JUST WANTED TO TELL YOU ABOUT OLD LADY HUDSON THEM," Willy shouted loud enough for her mother to hear.

She was glad he'd done that. Otherwise her mother might have asked why he was running after her. But sure enough, when she reached the porch her mother asked just that.

"What that boy Willy doin chasin after you? I see why you comin in here from school late every day. Git these heah buckets and git over there and git that water. Ruby Lee! Put them books down and take your school clothes off." She placed the buckets on the edge of the porch. "Heah, gimme them books. What you wanta do, leave them out heah for that damn dog to rip to pieces?"

Poochie handed her the books, then picked up the buckets and headed down the narrow path through the turnip patch towards the pump in back of Miss Fletcher's house.

"Look at you!" her mother was shouting. "Got yo mind so wrapped up in that damn boy, ain't even got a 'good evenin' for people."

Poochie stopped and turned around to face her mother. "You didn't give me a chance to say good evenin." She was tempted to tell her mother that she wasn't thinking about Willy, that instead she was only wondering what Willy had to say about Old Lady Hudson. But she didn't. She knew that whatever she said her mother would only make it look like she was indeed thinking about Willy. "How can you be thinkin bout somethin Willy said without thinkin bout Willy?" her mother had asked once after prying into Poochie's thoughts and discovering she was pondering over a riddle Willy had thrust upon her. So now when her mother asked her what she was thinking about, she simply said "nothing" and left it at that, knowing that whatever she said she was thinking about, one way or the other, her mother would see it as something to do with Willy. And as usual she was wrong.

"I just wanted to tell you bout Old Lady Hudson them." Even though it was Willy's voice she'd heard in her head, it was not Willy's voice she was thinking about but what was said. How could she explain that to a person like her mother? She saw Willy every day at school and every evening on her way from school, but she hadn't seen Old Lady and Old Man Hudson in two and a half months and she was always wondering how they were.

During the lunch hour at school she'd passed a bunch of students who were huddled around talking about some old couple who'd been burnt to death in their house. She got a real pang and was certain it was the Hudsons. But when she asked and discovered that the old couple who was dead had been killed because the old lady had left the gas stove on and returned to the kitchen some hours later to strike a match, she knew it was not the Hudsons. They didn't even have gas, much less a gas stove. They had a great big old wood-burning stove in the kitchen, a fireplace in the living room and a wood-burning heater in their bedroom. Upstairs in the bedrooms once occupied by their grown children there was no heat at all and the whole upper part of the house was shut up in the winter.

When Poochie had finished her dinner, washed the dishes and helped Ruby Lee with her lessons, she asked Lucille's permission to visit her friend Helen, who lived down the road a piece. Lucille's first answer was no, but when Poochie told her that they were having a spelling bee the next morning in class and that she and Helen had to study together, she changed her mind.

"You hurry yourself on down there but you'd better git back here fo dark."

"It's just about dark now, shoot, we won't have any time to study and Miss Brown is expecting me and Helen to beat Mrs. Cherry's class."

Whenever it was a question of Poochie's winning some contest, impressing her teacher Miss Brown or advancing herself in the eyes of others, Lucille did not gripe about it. But everything else was cause for complaints, especially in the area of courting and boys. She dreadfully feared that Poochie would get her mind all wrapped up in Willy or some other boy. She had hopes of Poochie becoming a schoolteacher or being a secretary in one of the big office buildings downtown but she knew that Poochie would never accomplish that if she got sidetracked with boys and stuff like that. And that Helen, well, she didn't even want Poochie having anything to do with her. But aside from Poochie, Helen was the smartest student in their class, even though she was as fast as a whip, and always had a bunch of boys hanging around her.

"If it's dark when y'all done finished, you better not come back down that road you yo'self. Git Helen and Elizabeth to walk you back here, and I mean Helen and Elizabeth and not all of them mannish-ass boys they always hanging around wit."

Poochie grabbed her speller and little concise dictionary and set out down the gravelly path in a trot. When she had turned the corner and was out of sight of her house she laid her heels in her back and did not stop running until she neared Helen's house. She hated having to lie to Lucille, but there was no other way. Now she would have to lie to Helen, because if she told Helen the truth and Helen "accidently" told her mother it would certainly get back to Lucille and Lucille would be even harder on her.

She was faced with a dilemma and did not know what to do. She had been in such predicaments before and had somehow gotten through them. She really hated that Helen was frivolous and even prejudiced too. That day at school when she had heard kids talking about the old couple who had been burnt to death in their house, she'd asked Helen about it.

"I ain't heard nothing bout any niggers getting burnt up. If they were white, well, it don't concern me."

But there was something about the way she had said that. Poochie was sure she was hiding something. If it was the Hudsons who'd been burnt to death she wouldn't tell me anyway, she thought, she had been so jealous when I was playing with Jill all summer. She even accused me of being a white-folks lover, and when that incident finally came up she was so glad. "You niggers gonna learn to stay in your place one day. Shit, what you wanta be washing yourself wit some white cracker for anyway?" Helen never got anything right and she never wanted to either.

Before she realized it Poochie had thought herself clean past Helen's house. She was not sure whether she'd been seen or not. But now that she was safely out of their sight, she didn't care. She laid her heels in her back again and directed all

her energies towards reaching the Hudsons' house
before dark. She was sure she couldn't make it
though, for the Hudsons lived every bit of two
miles from Helen's house.

After running about a mile or so, she was completely out of breath. She slowed down and let her
mind wander back to the last time she'd seen
the Hudsons.

It was the Fourth of July weekend and she and
Jill, Sally and Ruby Lee were all playing out under
the big oak tree in the back of the Hudsons' house.
They had been playing in the dirt and were very
dirty. It was almost time for Lucille to be leaving
with Ruby Lee and Poochie, when Old Lady Hudson came out back where they were playing.
When she saw that they were all extremely dirty,
she ushered them all into the kitchen where she had
the two tin washtubs steaming with hot water. She
asked Poochie and Jill to take cold water from the
tap and cool the water down. Poochie did so but
had no idea that she and Ruby Lee would be join-
ing Jill and Sally in the bath. Usually when it was
time for Sally and Jill to have their bath, they were
just leaving for home.

"Miss Hudson, I kin give them chaps of mine
their bath at home," Lucille protested when she
came in and saw all four of them standing naked
and Old Lady Hudson about to bathe them all in
the tubs together.

100

"You must be pretty tired already," Old Lady Hudson said. "It's nothing wrong with them having their bath here. You can rest when you get home."

Since Betsy and Bud were in town shopping, Lucille agreed there was nothing wrong with it. Even so, she insisted that Poochie and Ruby Lee share one tub and Sally and Jill the other. But Jill refused to bathe with Sally and insisted on sharing her tub with Poochie, and Old Lady Hudson agreed that it was all right.

They were all sitting there soaping each other's backs and sniggering down when in popped Betsy and Bud. First they just stood there with their eyes bulging out, seeing their little lily-white daughters sitting there sharing bubbles with two little pickaninnies, certainly an act over and far beyond the call of duty.

"Out! Out!" Betsy shouted, snatching Ruby Lee out of the tub. "Mama, whose idea was this?"

Just then Lucille ran in. "Take yo hands off my gal," she shouted. "It ain't her fault. Miss Hudson done said it was all right and I ain't seen nothing wrong wit it. It all in you dirty head."

"You take these little . . ." Betsy said, swinging at Lucille and missing her. Lucille grabbed her by the neck and they were down on the floor rolling between the two tubs. Old Lady Hudson fainted, ending the brawl between Lucille and Betsy.

Bud and Betsy carried Old Lady Hudson into

the living room and rested her on the sofa. Lucille got Ruby Lee and Poochie dressed and left. That'd happened two and a half months ago. The last time Poochie or any of them had seen the Hudsons.

As she neared the high bank leading to the Hudsons' house, she laid her heels in her back again for it was now almost dark. Once she'd reached it she stopped and just about crawled up the bank on all fours. She had no intention of going in; she just wanted to make sure that it was not the Hudsons who'd been burnt to death. When she reached the top she fell flat on her stomach. Then she looked and saw only the barn in the distance and the woods behind it. There was no house. She looked down at the ground and saw only a rectangular burnt-out patch in the grass where the house once stood.

"Oh! Oh, my God! It was the Hudsons. They must of got a gas stove. . . . Ooooh . . . Mama knew, I know she knew and so did Helen."

It was as if the house, the old couple and everything about them had vanished. She cried there on that bank until it was completely dark. Then she tucked her speller and little concise dictionary under her arm and headed home.